ISBN-13: 9780692017326
LCCN: 2011902758

Since the beginnings of human intelligence and speech, tales have been handed down from adults to children; many of these seemingly capricious parables contained messages, valuable recipes for surviving in society and the physical world. They are known as fables, and many of them are repeated again and again over time and in almost every culture.

Fables are one of the important beginnings for construction of the moral compass pointing to the future.

CONTENTS

THE GRASSHOPPER AND THE ANT

From early May, through every day,
the Grasshopper would sing and play.
The frugal Ant, as you must know,
was busy collecting food to show,
when all the ground was under snow.

As autumn came when cold winds blow,
Grasshopper said to Ant, "You know,
to tell you the truth, my dear,
I'm a little short this year.

"If you will lend me half your store,
next summer I'll repay you more."
Ant replied, "Sorry to see you so dismayed,
but while I worked you sang and played.

"Now finding food has no chance.
May I suggest you take up dance!"

Finish up your work each day,
before you think of fun and play.

1

THE SCORPION AND THE FROG

Walking along a bank one day,
a dangerous Scorpion was heard to say,
"If only I could find some way,
to cross this river here today."

        Whereupon he came upon
        a happy Frog who swam along,
        as easy as a floating ball.
        "I say there, Frog," he stood up tall,

"Let me climb upon your back,
then you can take me over there,
since nature gave you what I lack,
to swim all day without a care."

        "Whoa!" said Frog, "Ya think I'm daft?
        To use my body for a raft,
        and haul a cargo such as you,
        one quick stick could kill us two!"

"Oh no!" said Scorpion most sincere,
"I'm not ungrateful, do not fear."
And after some discussion more,
the two set out for the distant shore.

        Sure enough, as Frog foretold,
        midway the river, deep and cold,
        Scorpion panicked, stabbed his friend.
        And as they sank before the end,

Frog cried, "Alas my friend,
now we have no future!"
"Can't help it," said Scorpion.
"I'm afraid it's just my nature!"

Change someone against his will, he'll have the same opinion still.

THE FOX AND THE CROW

High on a branch in a tall oak tree,
sat a Crow, whose beak held dear,
a piece of cheese. And he could see,
there from his perch if one came near.

But down below there lurked a Fox,
as wily a creature as ever walked.
Said he, "You there who's shining locks
adorn this forest." And on he talked,

of beauty and talent and all the rest,
of shimmering coats and lovely feet.
Crow puffed up and swelled his breast,
believing now he was so neat.

Then finally Fox said with paw to ear,
"Throughout the forest it's said to hear,
your lovely voice so loud and clear,
that even the nightingale's no peer."

At last Crow could stand no more.
He opened his beak and with a snore,
cracked the air with a noise so vile,
that small birds hid for many a mile.

And when he did, fell to the ground,
his piece of cheese, and in one bound,
Fox sprang forth and gobbled up
that bite meant for poor Crow's sup.

For every flatterer you see, a flattered fool there be, let not that fool be thee.

THE COUNTRY MOUSE AND THE CITY MOUSE

Country Mouse, while in the city,
met his likeness smart dressed and witty,
who said, "Dear boy, it's such a pity,
to find you thus so lean and gritty.
    "Come along today with me.
    We'll dine on things you'll never see,
    stuck as you are living in a tree."
And off they went to a mansion grand,
City and Country Mouse, hand in hand.
    Said Country Mouse, really impressed,
    "All this food, I'd never have guessed!"
    But just as they sat down to eat,
    there came a noise like running feet.
Then a scratch outside their door,
and after that a terrible roar!
    A look of horror crossed the face,
    of City Mouse, who quit his place.
    He brought his finger to his lip,
    said, "Quiet now, we'll give the slip."
"To what, to what?" Country Mouse declared,
"Do you always eat your food this scared?"
"Only when the cat's around.
Quiet now, don't make a sound!"
    "Well, thanks again for your good cheer,
    but if you don't mind I'm out of here.
    My fare in the country may be lean,
    but I've never seen a thing so mean."
Just as fast as his feet could roam,
he headed for his country home.
He thanked his stars for his rotten tree,
and hoped that he would never again see,
a city, grand food, and such misery.

All that glitters is not gold, and all the truth is rarely told.
If you're content with what you've got, never wish for another's lot.

7

THE FOX AND THE STORK

As Fox sat down to eat one day,
he noticed a Stork had turned his way.
Said Stork to Fox, "What a terrible day,
I've found no food in any way.

"I say, could you share your fare,
with a hungry Stork?"
To which the Fox put down his fork,
tossed his head and said, "Sit there!"

Fox gave in to Stork's wish,
and down they sat to rice and fish.
The only trouble, as Stork soon learned,
was how his appetite had been spurned.

Wily Fox, who ate and ate,
served stork's meal upon a plate,
so flat, in fact, that Stork's long bill
could catch no food—he's hungry still!

Then Fox said, "If you're all through,
I'll lick your plate as clean as new."
Stork looked on in disbelief,
as wily Fox, the little thief,
ate all his dinner too!

When several months passed away,
and fortunes changed, as they may,
there sat Stork as he supped one day.
He noticed that Fox had come to say,

"By the way, I'm a little short today.
Could you spare a morsel for a friend?
To you I shall not pretend.
I've not eaten since weekend!"

"With great pleasure!" said Stork,
and as a gesture gave Fox a fork.
But when the two sat down to eat,
what Stork gave Fox was no treat.

Stork served dinner to his friend,
in a longneck jug with one small end!

Carefully give out what you may, for it all comes back to you one day.

THE WOLF AND THE DOG

A drought so bad had parched the land,
that even the forest was barely sand.
A poor Wolf, who staggered with a sway,
was lean and hungry with great dismay.
                    Dazed with hunger he walked all around,
                    until at last wandered into town.
                    A noise he heard dispersed his fog,
                    and before his eyes there stood a Dog.

Dog was clean and clipped and fed,
and close by him was a padded bed.
Between his paws was a juicy bone,
which Wolf saw and breathed a moan.
                    "Say," said Dog as he chattered on,
                    "Is it true that you are all alone?
                    And never know from day to day,
                    if you're to eat? Or so they say.

"Three squares a day and a juicy treat,
like this one here between my feet.
I could never live like you,
wondering if there's something left to chew."
                    Wolf then asked, with a suspicious air,
                    "And what's one do for such a fare?"
                    "Oh, for all that it's not much;
                    a little of this and such and such.

"Chase away all bums you see,
and vagrant cats go up a tree.
Be at human's beck and call,
take cold baths, that's bout all."
                    Wolf then noticed on Dog's neck,
                    a scar, no hair, though just a speck.
                    "What's that disease around your neck?"
                    and Dog replied, "It's just a speck.

"It comes from when I run away,
but the length of chain is out of play."
"You're chained!" cried Wolf with great dismay.
"Only during the day, when they're away."
                    Then Wolf sighed and with a sway,
                    bid Dog goodbye and went his way.

As harsh to you as it might seem, food is second to freedom's dream.

11

THE FROG WHO WANTED TO BE A HORSE

In a secluded lake there lived two Frogs,
happily jumping from lilies to logs.
By chance there came a Horse their way,
to get a drink from the lake today.

The Frogs had lived so long apart,
that this new vision gave them a start.
They stared and stared with considerable awe,
not believing what they saw.

"How beautiful he is!" exclaimed one Frog.
"His massive size and muscled limb."
"Poo!" said the other Frog, jumped off his log,
saying on a whim, "I can be as big as him."

And to prove his point, he drank from the lake.
He drank and drank, and make no mistake,
he did get bigger the more he drank,
so much, in fact, he became a tank.

Then finally there came a sound,
fairly heard the world around.
Frog had exploded, against his will,
and that timid horse is running still.

Envy is a bottomless lake, once you start it's hard to shake.
You drink and drink, like this poor frog, and in the end there's only fog.

THE HARE AND THE TORTOISE

Spare a moment, you over there,
and I'll tell the story of Tortoise and Hare.
It seems that on one summer day,
an ambling Tortoise made his way,
with a slow and steady pace.

All at once, from nowhere,
sprang a Hare, who said, "You there!
Of all the critters in field and stream,
you're the slowest I've ever seen."
But Tortoise continued to keep his pace.

Hare spun around and round,
he even jumped up and down.
Then said Hare, with grimaced face,
"Tell ya what, let's have a race!"
But Tortoise merely kept his pace.

"What's the matter, you got no pride?"
Hare circled round from side to side.
Said the Tortoise with no change of face,
"OK, pest, let's have your race!"
But still he did not break his pace.

Hare sped off with a happy face,
leaving the Tortoise at his slow pace.
He ran along so fast and light,
that very soon he was out of sight.
But Tortoise just kept to his pace.

Believing that Tortoise was far behind,
said Hare, "I'll rest now, he won't mind.
Ah yes," said Hare, "A shady tree.
If Tortoise comes now I will see."
And Tortoise continued to keep the pace.

Hare fell asleep; time came at last,
when Tortoise quietly ambled past.
When Hare awoke, the sun had gone.
He bolted on the road alone!
But Tortoise won the race! He'd kept the pace!

It is said the race is to the swift, but the pace makes the race, if you catch my drift.

THE LION AND THE RAT

A mighty Lion while hunting one day,
spied a Rat who'd come out to play.
With one swift move of his great paw,
he pulled Rat up unto his jaw.

"Wait!" cried the Rat, "Sir noble knight,
my sad body is but one small bite.
I'm well below your usual fare,
just skin and bones—mostly hair.

"But if you will spare my life today,
the time will come when I'll repay
this gesture of your good intent."
So Rat was freed, and off he went.

The years passed on, and Lion grew old,
no longer courageous, quick, and bold.
Then one sad day, in early May,
a trap he sprung to his dismay.

A net of rope, close knit and strong,
poor Lion howled the whole night long.
From far away Rat heard the plea,
and ran toward his friend to see.

When Rat arrived and saw the net,
he said, "Dear friend, please do not fret,
I've got a plan to free you yet!"
Then began in earnest to chew the net.

In no time at all the net did fall,
and Lion was free to go.
Though Rat was small,
just so you know,
he'd freed the mighty Lion!

Good deeds are like seeds you sow, when they will bloom you never know.

THE BOY WHO CRIED WOLF

In a little town a bit north of here,
most folks lived in constant fear,
of Wolves from the nearby woods.
With all eyes peeled and dogs well heeled,
they guarded all their goods.

There was a Boy in this small town,
who lived and breathed to be a clown.
And when all the town were fast asleep,
he'd cry, "Wolf! Wolves in the sheep!"

When the town folks heard him shout,
each and every one came out,
to drive the Wolves away.
Then that bad Boy would simply say,
"You silly geese, there are no Wolves today."

This went on and on 'til late fall.
And as always no Wolves at all.
Finally, when he began to call,
no one came, no one at all.

Then one day, while on his way,
he noticed the bushes began to sway.
"What could this be?" He tried to see!
"There it goes, behind that tree!"

Then all at once from a thick brush,
a real Wolf jumped with quite a rush.
With sharp teeth bared and hungry mean,
Wolf fixed the Boy with a steady gleam.

The Boy cried, "Wolf!" with all his might,
but no help came from town that night.
Folks who listened to his noise
just grinned, and said, "Boys will be boys."

Do not say what isn't true, the Wolf's next meal just could be you.

19

TWO MULES

What everyone knows, or it would seem,
is that Mules are ornery and mean.
And to work well as a pair,
is something so rare,
you might say it seldom is seen.

> A farmer had two Mules, as you see.
> No more hardheaded beasts there could be.
> He tied them together,
> thinking that now on a tether,
> they'd walk around free but not flee.

Having done this he departed,
and several day's trip he then started.
What no one knew then was that fate would extend,
more days than he did first intend.

> At first the Mules just stood still,
> for both had eaten their fill.
> But as time wore on thin,
> hunger set in,
> and a search for food did begin.

For days they pulled and they tugged,
'til at last they sat down and just shrugged.
Between two hay stacks in defeat,
though both wanted to eat,
each was short by ten feet!

> An Owl on a nearby post,
> said, "Guys, don't mean to boast.
> But what I would say,
> if both pulled the same way,
> you might get some hay down today!"

"I get it," they brayed with delight,
then both moved left and then right.
What began as a fight
ended alright,
Now there is no hay in sight.

To break a twig is quick and fun, but with several together it can't be done.

21

THE CAT'S PAW

A Cat and Monkey by the fire one night,
watched folks roast nuts to their delight.
To their chagrin a nut fell in, just barely out of sight.

Each in turn gave it his best, but despite their
fruitless pluck,
though all tried hard to brave the fire, not one
had any luck.
And after a while and many tries, all admitted
that they were stuck.

All at once that clever Monk grabbed the Kitty's paw.
What came next was beyond belief; while all stood there in awe,
with Cat's paw, Monk raked out the nut. And that is what we saw.

The scent of hair was in the air,
and Cat made quite a yelp,
but Monk sat there with just a stare,
and said, "Thanks for all your help!"

If others use you for their gain,
then who is crazy and who is sane?

23

THE BAMBOO AND THE OAK

A Bamboo grew to considerable size,
but was shaded by an Oak in whose eyes,
he was but an ornery weed.

Oak would chide Bamboo each day,
with snide remarks, like he'd say,
"I can't believe you have no seed!

"And if any bird of size came 'round,
he'd bend your trunk down to the ground.
To sit on you is no treat, indeed."

This went on for many years.
The big Oak's talk just brought on tears.
Bamboo thought, "Am I never to be freed?"

Then one night a cyclone blew.
A great wind came upon the two.
And sadly one was lost indeed.

Bamboo just swayed down to the ground,
but that mighty Oak came crashing down.
Here's a serious lesson you must heed.

Strength alone is not enough, flexibility makes you tough.

25

THE MICE AND THE CAT

A group of Mice had gathered one day,
to see if there was any way,
to foil the local Cat.

After much discussion and much noise,
the smartest and fattest said, "Boys,
our biggest problem is knowing where he's at.

"I mean, you know, I'm so slow,
that when Cat is on the go,
I'm stuck at home and that's that!

"If only there was some clever way,
to tell if Cat is home today."
And after that he sat.

"How's about we scatter out, and when he comes we'll holler."
"That's no good," said another. "I know, let's make a collar!"
And they all agreed on that.

"On that collar we'll tie a bell,
then that way we can tell,
where that fat Cat is at!"

The whole group laughed and worked with glee.
They finally held it up to see.
Then all at once they all just sat.

"Why so sad?" asked one lad.
Another said, "Oh we've been had.
Who will put it on the Cat?!"

All good plans of mice and men are zero if they're not brought in.

HORSE FOR SALE

A farmer rode his horse to sell,
with his son who walked.
Both were happy, you could tell,
by how they laughed and talked.

All at once they met someone,
with a grimaced face,
who said, "Why should you ride upon?
The lad should take your place!"

So off he jumped onto the ground,
to give his son a ride.
And now the farmer walked around,
along the horse's side.

The next they met said, "I declare!
Must one walk, why don't you share?"
So up he went behind his son,
and with that you'd think them done.

But then a third man said, "I'll give you my advice.
To treat that beast in such a way just isn't very nice!"
To make it short, for time now lacks, they ended up with that poor horse,
carried on their backs!

Free advice is far and wide,
but your own good sense is your best guide.

KNOWLEDGE AND WISDOM

In a town far, far away,
lived five boys, good friends they say.
Four were learned, the fifth deemed thick,
though despite no learning his mind was quick.

>They call it common sense, you know,
>slow with books but plenty of go.
>This poor lad had not the means,
>to formally learn what's taught, it seems.

On the road together one day,
a dying Lion lay in their way.
"With our great knowledge," one learned did say,
"We can raise this Lion here today."

>"Just a minute!" cried their quick friend,
>"If you revive this Lion, and then,
>'twas hunger that made his puny state,
>he's simply weak cause he's not ate!"

"Well, who are you to counsel us?
We're all learned, what's your fuss?
With our great minds and foresight,
 just our knowledge can put him right."

>"Since you four learned now all agree,
>just give me time to climb that tree.
>And while your knowledge you display,
>I'll just hide there far away."

As quick one climbed up this tree,
the others worked and worked with glee.
At last the Lion was full awake,
but his hungry mien caused all to quake.

>From his safe perch and with great chagrin,
>he watched Lion do the others in.
>And after Lion left with his belly filled,
>Quick descended forever chilled.

To have great knowledge is good indeed,
but knowledge without wisdom is just a seed.

31

THE THREE PIGS

Three brother Pigs had come of age.
Two were foolish, but one was sage.
When time came to build a home,
each decided he'd make his own.

> The first Pig used what he easily saw.
> His work was puny, his house just straw.
> When strong winds blew,
> as you know they do,
> this lazy Pig's house was blown askew!

The second Pig was full of tricks.
He built his house entirely of sticks!
But there came a flood one fateful day,
and washed his house entirely away!

> The third Pig used neither straw nor sticks,
> but built his house of strong red bricks.
> Though the work was harder, that's to say,
> that Pig's house still stands today!

Things easily obtained are easily lost;
what's obtained without effort is worth what it cost.

THE CHICKEN AND THE WHEAT

A Hen one day scratched in the ground,
for food, you know, and what she found,
were several grains of wheat.
At first she thought, "Ah, now I'll eat!
But then I think, on second thought,
if we can plant these seeds I've got,
in the fall we'll have a lot!"
And she called her friends to the spot.

Hen said, "If you will help me plant these seeds,
then in the fall they'll fill our needs."
But of all that crowd that stood around,
not one peep, not a single sound.
"OK," said Hen, "If that's the case,
it's up to me to take your place."
And off she went to work alone.

In the fall the plants she'd sown
were waist high and fully grown.
Though all the others milled around,
when help was asked, not a sound.
And off she went to work alone.

And when that wheat was taken in,
she asked them all with a timid grin,
"Who will help me grind this wheat?"
But all she heard was shuffling feet.
So off she went to work alone.

With that flour she baked some bread.
The aroma they smelled for miles, it's said.
And when the others crowded around,
she dropped her head and made no sound.
And off she went to eat her bread alone.

Don't expect to share the bread, if others work and you're in bed.

THE EMPEROR'S NEW CLOTHES

There once was a powerful man,
known as the Emperor Asham.
Even his foes, as everyone knows,
admired the cut of his clothes.

> As many years had passed on,
> bits of his mind seemed to be gone.
> Then early one morn, as if he'd been shorn,
> he appeared like the day he was born.

All of his cronies in court,
from fear refused to report,
what everyone saw and everyone knows.
The Emperor was wearing no clothes!

> His nobles in turn came to say,
> "How well you are dressed up today.
> Are these clothes new? We'd like to convey,
> we've never seen you dressed in this way!"

Then from the crowd there appeared,
a small boy, and as everyone feared,
said, "Sir, let me say, you're quite a display!
You have not a stitch on today!"

> "What is the meaning of this?"
> said the poor man with a hiss.
> "Of all standing here who pretend to be dear,
> my shocking condition you missed?"

Then with the wave of his hand,
all of his Yes Men he banned.
He scooped up the boy like he was a toy,
and put him in charge of the land.

To tell the truth, one must be bold, but when you do, it's as good as gold.

SUN AND WIND

The Great North Wind blew up a fuss,
and said to Sun, "Of the two of us,
I'm the stronger one by far!"
           Sun said, "Just because you topple trees,
           and freeze lost Bees below their knees,
           does not make you a bloomin' czar!

"Your bleak and nasty days,
 your cold and frigid ways,
just show me the bully that you are."
           "OK!" said Wind, "Set me a test,
           so I can show you who is the best."
           And the two prepared in earnest to go spar.

Sun replied, "See that man who wears a vest?
We'll take him to be our test,
on condition that you do not harm or mar.
           "The first to make him shed his vest,
           will be the winner of the test.
           If you really think that you are up to par."

With that Wind laughed and with a grin,
 like a cyclone, sucked air in,
swaying all the trees for near and very far.
           Then at last he blew a blast,
           of frozen air that made all gasp,
           and iced the trees like a shimmering star.

The poor man shook down to the ground,
but pulled his vest more tightly around,
to shield himself from the icy jar.
           Sun said, "Good show, old man! But not enough!
           You see at last you're not so tough.
           Now it is my turn to spar!"
           He gently beamed out his warm ray.
           The man now welcomed this lovely day,
           removed his vest, and skipped along his way.

Some think that force is always best, but gentle persuasion wins the test.

A BIGGER BONE

A dog was scrounging for food one day,
but they'd all say, "Not today, go away!"

> When, at last, did he perceive,
> a juicy bone, do you believe.

He snatched it up, and with a bound,
made for the woods, least he be found.

> Now to reach the woods he'd pass a stream,
> obliged to cross on a narrow beam.

Midway across on this perilous trek,
a vision caused him to turn his neck.

> What he saw, with his own eyes,
> was another bone of enormous size.

He opened his mouth to grab that bone,
but caught just water, and that alone.

> To his amazement this disguise,
> was just a trick played on his eyes.

And as he watched with great dismay,
his own true bone was swept away.

> Now all that was left was just a sigh,
> and one big tear in his right eye.

If you are happy with your lot,
don't let go of what you've got.

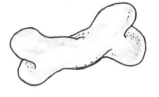

THE FLYING TORTOISE

A Tortoise, with envy, watched the sky,
with a pitiful longing and wondered why,
he himself could not fly.

        This went on for many years,
        when at last, with many fears,
        he approached an Eagle, his eyes in tears.

"I say, Sir Eagle, king of the sky,
if you will take me way up high,
then I too can try to fly!"

        "I'd like to help, I won't deny,"
        said the Eagle as he blinked an eye.
        "But I'm not sure a Tortoise can fly.

"If you insist I guess we might."
He grabbed the Tortoise with talons tight,
and carried him up to an awesome height.

        "Drop me now!" the Tortoise cried.
        "Well, spread your legs!" the Eagle sighed.
        And down Tortoise fell in suicide!

Down went Tortoise, and in a flash,
he hit the ground with such a splash,
that nothing remained—not one eyelash!

To be you is not a sin,
but copying others can do you in.

THE MOUSE AND THE FROG

A Mouse, on his way to town,
was obliged to pass around,
a lake wherein there lived a Frog.

And each and every time he went,
the Frog his copious greetings sent,
from atop a nearby log.

"G'day!" he'd say while going each way,
and Mouse replied with the same "G'day!"
whether it was clear or in a heavy fog.

Then one day while on his way,
Mouse heard the Froggy say,
"Come swim with me, if you feel so disposed."

Mouse replied, "I do not swim,
as well as you can on a whim."
"I know," said Frog. "It's just as I supposed.

"Tie this cord around your arm,
I'll attach it to my leg so there's no harm."
Mouse conceded, and into the lake he nosed.

All went well at the start,
but when they reached the deepest part,
that treacherous Frog to the bottom dove!

The frantic Mouse kicked and fluttered,
'til at last he surfaced and sputtered,
with the Frog still tightly hove.

A passing Hawk, drawn to the fuss,
said, "Look what luck has brought to us,
a tasty morsel!" and with talons bared he dove.

But when he plucked the Mouse—Surprise!
A Frog attached to please his eyes.
(To Hawks, Frogs are a rare and delicious prize.)

He dropped the Mouse and grabbed the Frog.
Poor Mouse fell safely onto a log,
grateful that he had narrowly missed his demise.

Whether it's by thought or sword, treachery is its own reward.

THE TURTLE AND THE MONKEY

In Africa, some time ago, a hunter in the brush,
found a large Turtle, which he picked up with a rush.
"Oh boy!" he cried with sheer delight, "It's Turtle stew today!"
"Hold on!" Turtle went on to say. "Stew's not the gourmet way!

"First you get a rope and attach it to my arm, this way,
Then loop it over a tree limb and hoist me up today.
Let me hang there for three days, no more, no less, to start.
That way all internal poisons will have a chance to part.

"Then find a rock both large and flat and heat it in the fire.
Place me on it, but take me off just as I expire."
The Turtle was relieved a bit when the hunter did as told.
He'd bought some time, but now he'd need a plan for growing old.

Late on the second day, eyes closed, as he thought and thought,
a Monkey sat before him and said, "What is this you've got?"

All at once the Turtle began to dance with a happy mien.
"Why so happy and why the dance?" said Monkey, at what he'd seen.
"I'm rehearsing for my marriage day!" the Turtle went on to say.
"I'm to marry the chief's daughter in just one more single day!"

"How absurd!" replied the Monkey. "To think that a creature like you,
should presume to be royalty when I'm the better of us two!"
With that the Monkey untied the rope and threw the Turtle away.
He then attached it to his own arm in just the very same way.

The Monkey danced the whole day long. Then just before the night,
the hunter came to gather his prize. Turtle watched safely out of sight.
"What has happened here? I can't believe my eyes!
The Turtle's become a dancing Monkey. Now there's a real surprise.
My heart was set on Turtle stew,
but Monkey stew will have to do!"

If you want to steal another's lot, be sure you know what it is you've got.

THE DOVE AND THE BEE

By a pool, up in a tree,
sat a Dove upon a limb.
From his place he could see,
a poor Bee who'd fallen in.

"Why the struggle and chagrin?"
said Dove to Bee, who'd fallen in.
Bee replied, "It's not a whim.
Of all my talents, I cannot swim!"

Dove was stunned beyond belief,
but to help poor Bee he tossed a leaf.
Bee climbed on with great relief,
shook his wings and sighed, "Good grief!"

The sun was hot and with a breeze,
soon Bee was dry and full at ease.
He flapped his wings and buzzed away,
said to the Dove, "My thanks today!"

After some weeks had passed away,
as Bee was gathering food one day,
he saw his friend up in a tree.
But to his horror he could see,

a gun aimed at his friend!
Bee dove hard, just like the wind,
stung that hunter square on his back.
The gun went off with an awesome "Crack!"

It missed its mark, and in the end,
Bee had chanced to save his friend.
Dove had safely flown away,
and they're still good friends to this very day.

Good deeds done can give a boost; what's given out comes home to roost.

THE DOLPHIN AND THE APE

Years ago, one night at sea,
a ship was driven hard to lee.
All went down in a swirling mist,
and a traveling circus was on the list.

> A passing Dolphin heard all the raves,
> and swam with haste through crashing waves.
> When at last he reached the spot,
> he spied a man—or so he thought!

Just so you know, and I'm sure it's right,
Dolphins are partial to Man's plight.
When any man goes down at sea,
a Dolphin who's close his friend will be.

> So it was that stormy night.
> What Dolphin saw, a man in sight,
> was nothing more in his misty gape,
> than a different primate, a hairy Ape!

"Jump aboard, my troubled friend!
I'll take you ashore to land's end!"
As lightening flew with a terrible crack,
Ape climbed upon Dolphin's back.

> On closer look Dolphin knew
> this hairy figure seemed askew.
> Ape insisted that he was a man,
> but Dolphin began to smell a scam.

"I say!" said Dolphin to his charge,
"You look like a human, you're just as large.
But something tells me it's just not true.
To me your face is something new!

> "Tell me now, if you're to boast,
> what one food d'ya like the most?"
> Ape replied then with a boast,
> "Banana! That is what I like the most!"

Dolphin now angry that he'd been used,
(though Ape persisted with his ruse)
ceased to his charge a friend to be,
turned and dropped him out to sea.

Don't pretend what you cannot be, or chances are you'll drown at sea.

51

A CROW'S LAMENT

The blackest Crow I ever saw,
sat in a tree in constant awe,
of a Swan floating on a nearby lake.

            "To be just as white as snow!"
            with envy thought that black Crow.
            "What I would not this day give or take!"

At last he thought he knew the path.
"That Swan doesn't just take a bath.
His whole world's a tub, for goodness sake!

            "I'm sure if I could bathe just so,
            my coat can be as white as snow!"
            With that he swelled and gave a great big shake.

He left his perch there high and dry,
with a single thought in his mind's eye,
to change his home to dwelling on the lake.

            At first it seemed to be a go,
            though how funny to see a floating Crow,
            and all the others felt pity for his sake.

The problem is, as you might know,
all Crows' feathers are made just so,
with not the oil to float upon a lake.

            Crow sputtered and sank and lost his wind,
            but a passing Swan became his friend,
            and hauled him up from the bottom of the lake.

To change your nature might be your dream,
but it can't be done by a change of scene.

WRONG WAY

I met a man on the road headed,
a southern way.
When I asked his destination he
had this to say:

> "I'm going to the city that is
> along this way."
> I replied, "The city's north, not south,
> even if you say."

"I have fast horses to speed me,
quickly on my way."
"Fast or slow makes no difference. You're
headed wrong, I say!"

> "I have lots of money; that's always
> been the way."
> "Even with your money the city is
> north, I say!"

"My driver is the very best. He should
know his way."
Finally in desperation I had only
this to say:

> "Fast horses, great wealth, and the
> best driver are speeding you
> wrong today!"

Great possessions, as they say, are a lovely sight,
but when you're wrong, you're wrong, and they
do not make you right!

TASSY

There was a Tasmanian Devil,

who, when spinning, made everything level.

It's from ambition, I fear,

he spun up his own ear,

and now that

poor Devil

is level

!

What's the point? If you should ask...
Don't let your reach exceed your grasp!

THE CROW WHO WANTED TO BE AN EAGLE

As a crow was soaring high up one day,
he witnessed an Eagle make quite a display.
Eagle dove at the ground with great speed,
and plucked from a herd a lamb like a seed.

Eagle flew off with his prey held so tightly.
Crow was impressed at what he had done sprightly.
He thought to himself, "Now there's a neat trick,
a way to get dinner quietly and quick."

So he hoisted himself up to a thousand feet,
and turned to imitate that Eagle's neat feat.
When Crow hit the herd with his silly scam,
instead of a lamb he hit a hundred pound ram.

Try as he may he could not budge his prey.
To make matters worse and woe to his day,
Crow's claws were entangled in that ram's wool.
Now you can guess who looked like a fool.

The shepherd was drawn by noise to the site,
as Crow tried to leave with all of his might.
Now Crow spends his days with that shepherd's boy,
with a cord on his leg like some pitiful toy.

Should you crave to wear another's skin,
be sure you know the game you're in.

THE HAWK AND THE SPARROWS

A group of Sparrows were harried each day,
by a vicious and hungry bird of prey.
But Sparrows are quick and agile, they say,
so every time he swooped on them, they just flew away.

After weeks and weeks of constant trying,
Hawk, from hunger, was close to dying.
All his efforts were reduced to spying,
on all the food that he was eyeing.

A plan at last he conceived.
"What if these morsels can be deceived?
Let's see what invention can be believed!"
And from these thoughts he was much relieved.

He approached the group, but not too close,
and with an air of extreme and royal verbose,
saying, "For your good, make me your king,
then I'll protect you from everything!"

At first the group was filled with fright,
but these poor Sparrows were not too bright.
So all agreed with great delight,
since now they'd never have to fight.

As the time went on and on,
they disappeared one by one.
Hawk grew fatter by a lot,
but no one saw him leave his spot.

The last one left became suspicious,
but to the Hawk he looked delicious.
Then Hawk said so convincingly,
"For your own good, stay close to me."

If you give or sell your destiny, a life of peril you'll surely see.

FOX AND THE TIGER

The Fox is as crafty an animal as you will ever see.
He sneaks at night and steals your chicks and will not let you be.
Here is a story to make the point about this clever fellow.
He cheated death by guile and brass; call him never yellow.
Napping one day he was caught by a Tiger of fierce hunger, and mean.

"Whoa!" said Fox. "Better think twice if you want to make me lunch!
I'm a messenger for the gods. Don't want to anger that bunch!
My power is so well known that all who see me shirk."
But Tiger, unconvinced, just laughed and shook him with a jerk.
"That's quite a story," said the Tiger. "Your power remains to be seen.

"If you can prove to me this folly, then I will let you go."
"Then take me over there." said Fox. "Other animals will know.
Hold me high for all to see, then roar to get attention.
Yell out loud, 'What d'ya think of this' in case I forgot to mention."
The Tiger did as he was told and approached a group of fifteen.

He laughed out loud, but as agreed, held up Fox for all to see.
When he roared (as Fox knew they would) they all began to flee.
Tiger then dropped the Fox, scratched his head and said, "I'll be!"
He shouted, "If you're watching, I've set your messenger free!"

Though the one who's singing may not be strong,
it's the power behind him who writes the song
and you might be wise to follow along.

THE LION'S DISPUTE

Two Lions were hunting alone one day,
each one on his separate way.
What makes this story unique, you say,
is that each one stalked the same poor prey.

                When at last they sprang to kill,
                what happened next provoked a chill.
                The two collided in mid air,
                with a deafening noise and flying hair.

The prey was dead, make no mistake,
but not a portion could either take.
They pulled and tugged, roared and fought,
but in the end were overwrought.

                Of equal strength and equal air,
                both settled down to a hostile stare.
                Then finally just at day's last light,
                a passing Jackal saw their plight.

"A simple solution I have for you.
With my sharp teeth I'll cut in two,
this object of your long dispute."
And the Lions accepted without refute.

                When Jackal cut the meat in two,
                his idea of equal was a bit askew.
                One piece was large, the other small,
                and the shorted Lion roared, "Won't do at all!""

Then Jackal said, "Be calm and sit,
to even up I'll chew a bit."
You'll never guess what happened next.
He ate too much! Now the other perplexed,

                said, "Wait a minute, now he has more!"
                "Be calm," said Jackal, just as before,
                "I'll chew a little and even up."
                This scam continued 'til both Lions' sup,

Was eaten by Jackal!

The worst arrangement made between foes,
exceeds what any outsider knows.

THE FOX AND THE GRAPES

A Fox, while hunting for food one day, came upon some grapes.

How sweet and delicious they looked up there growing on an arbor.

A vision of many sizes and colors—big and little shapes.

But they grew so high that efforts to obtain them were just a futile labor.

Despite the repeated tries he made, no grapes for him today.

And when at last he gave it up he had this to say:

"I've skipped and hopped and jumped and leapt for better than an hour,

But not one grape has passed my lips—most likely they're too sour!"

Confront your failures with resolve and class.
Don't be petty by pretending they're crass.

A WOODSMAN'S REQUEST

Some time ago, when trees still talked,
a man approached a group of trees.
He asked that one give up a limb,
even begged them on his knees.

A selfish and thoughtless oak declared,
"I'll not give up one of mine,
but you may take one from that ash."
The others all agreed in chime.

As soon as the man had taken a limb,
he fashioned a handle for an axe.
He then began to chop them down,
'til none were left—and there's the facts!

It's bad enough to betray a friend,
but breaking unity brings everyone's end.

THE THOROUGHBRED

A sow with many pigs ambled along the road.

The piglets were running here and there, squirming all about.

And any hope of controlling them lay in serious doubt.

Coming from the opposite way a magnificent Thoroughbred strode.

The sow inquired, all puffed up, "How many are your get?"

"Just one colt, but very well bred. On him you can stake a bet!"

A single job done with thorough intent,
is superior to many mediocre sent!

WHY BATS LIVE IN CAVES

The birds and mammals had a great battle in
the dim and distant past.
But the Bat (duplicitous in body and character),
held out until the last,

To choose a side when the victory would emerge,
with a certainty he could see.
Then with little or no effort on his part a
victor he too could be.

At first it seemed that the mammals were winning,
so far as he could see
So Bat moved over to join that group,
to enjoy their victory.

But a rally ensued on the part of the birds, and
'twas birds that would endure.
When the Bat saw that he quickly switched sides,
now that he was sure.

The birds saw through his deceit, and so
did the mammals as well.
Now both sides shunned this deceiver since,
the entire world could tell,

That his only allegiance was to himself,
with only himself to save.
So he was banned to live hiding forever
in a cold and darkened cave!

If you always think, in time of need, of just yourself to save,
then you too like that Bat will end up in a cold and
darkened cave.

THE VALUE OF FLATTERY

A rich man, traveling home one day,
met a beggar coming his way.
The beggar bowed as low as he may,
saying, "Kind and handsome sir, I say,

could you spare a little offering today?"
And the rich man now had this to say:
"Well, let me see," the man replied.
"This full pouch, carried on my side,

is full of gold, bless my hide!"
And the beggar's eyes grew very wide.
The man continued, as if to chide,
"If I give you a third of what's inside,

would you flatter me well both far and wide?"
"I can't be sure," the beggar replied.
"Then what if half came to your side?
Would you now flatter me far and wide?"

"Half's a lot," the beggar sighed
"But not enough for far and wide!"
"Then if all my purse moved to your side?"
And now the beggar remarked so snide,

"With all your gold now on my side,
there's no more need to flatter!" he cried.

To have great wealth, now there's a thought,
but sincere feelings cannot be bought.

THE SQUIRREL AND THE BEAR

A Squirrel, though agile, lost his grip,
and fell at the feet of a Bear,
who snapped him up and licked his lip,
with a mean and grizzly stare.

> "Hold on!" cried Squirrel, "Now you just wait,
> you're not as strong as you think!
> What if I told you that I once ate
> one like you—black as ink?!"

Bear laughed so hard that he dropped his charge,
and said, "Now let us see!
If you can show me you're half so large,
then I will let you be."

> "What's the hardest thing you know?"
> said Squirrel, tiny claws still bared.
> "A rock's the hardest, I think so.
> Yes a rock!" the Bear declared.

"Can you hit one 'til it bleeds?"
the Squirrel went on to say.
And they found a rock hidden in the weeds,
which Bear hit—but no blood today!

> Squirrel smacked the rock with his tiny paw,
> and "blood" splashed all around
> (from a red berry hidden under his claw,
> he'd taken from the ground).

"Can you beat that? I thought you'd lose!"
said Bear with a puzzled look.
"Another test, my time to choose!"
so angry that he shook.

> "Kill a thing with just one blow!"
> But to his surprise Squirrel said yes!
> (Squirrels are not that strong, you know.)
> Squirrel went on, "Game's for me to guess."

"Kill an ant over there. They're crawling all around!"
And he assumed a cocky stance.
But each time Bear's slow paw hit the ground,
he missed the scurrying ants.

> Squirrel easily killed an ant with his quick and tiny paw.
> Bear gave a sigh of disbelief at what he now saw.
> "Today's your lucky day!" said Squirrel as he scurried up a tree.
> "Since I'm not hungry for Bear today, I will let you be!"

Strength has limits that one can measure, but resourceful wisdom is an unlimited treasure.

THE FOX AND THE GOAT

A Fox, while drinking from a well,
lost his grip, and down he fell.
The walls were slippery to his chagrin,
and each time he jumped he fell back in.

A thirsty Goat was passing by,
looked in the well and with a sigh,
asked of the Fox, "Is there enough to drink?"
"If you come down here, there's plenty I think."

The unsuspecting Goat jumped in.
But after he drank it occurred to him,
That he was stuck down in the well.
And with that thought he began to yell.

"Hold on!" said Fox, "I've got a plan.
Brace yourself against the wall,
then I'll crawl up and out to land.
Once I'm out I'll give you a hand."

Goat braced himself as Fox had said,
and Fox climbed out by use of Goat's head.
But once Fox was free he said, "Goodbye,"
and left poor Goat in the well to cry.

Beware of joining another's game.
It may be you stuck with the blame!

WISE BOOKS